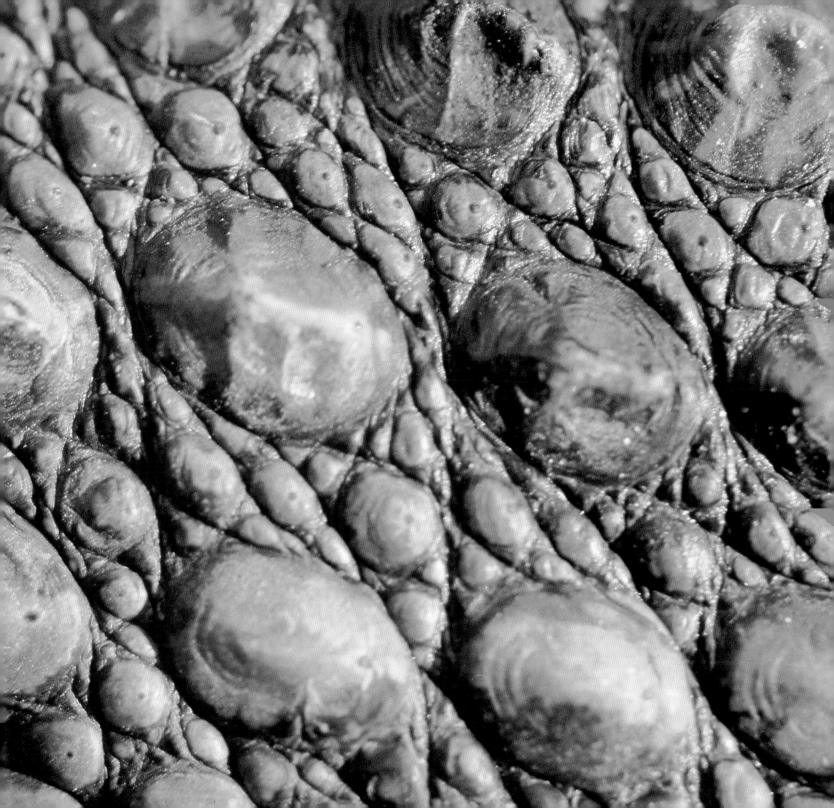

A Michael Neugebauer Book

First published in the United States, Canada, Great Britain, Australia,
and New Zealand in 1994 by North-South Books, an imprint of Nord-Süd Verlag AG.
First paperback edition published in 2000 by North-South Books.

Text and photographs copyright © 1993 by Mark Deeble and Victoria Stone
First published in Switzerland under the title Das Krokodil-Kinder-Buch
by Michael Neugebauer Verlag AG, Gossau Zürich.
The Animal Family series is supervised by biologist Sybille Kalas.

Distributed in the United States by North-South Books Inc., New York.

Deeble, Mark
[Krokodil-Kinder-Buch. English]
The crocodile family book / Mark Deeble, Victoria Stone.
(The Animal family series)
1. Crocodiles—Tanzania—Serengeti National Park—Juvenile literature.
[1. Crocodiles—Tanzania. 2. Serengeti National Park (Tanzania) 3. National parks
and reserves—Tanzania.] I. Stone, Victoria. II. Title. III. Series.
QL666.C925D4313 1994 597.98—dc 20 94-17262

A CIP catalogue record for this book is available from The British Library.
ISBN 1-55858-263-0 (trade edition) 10 9 8 7 6 5 4 3 2 1
ISBN 1-55858-264-9 (library edition) 10 9 8 7 6 5 4 3 2 1
ISBN 0-7358-1317-5 (paperback) 10 9 8 7 6 5 4 3 2 1
Printed in Italy

Mark Deeble

Victoria Stone

The Crocodile Family Book

NORTH-SOUTH BOOKS / NEW YORK / LONDON

Far away in Africa a small river called the Grumeti draws its water from the plains of Tanzania's Serengeti National Park and drains into Lake Victoria. The Grumeti lies just below the equator, so it's hot here all year long. There is no winter, but there are seasons—a wet season, when it rains a lot, and a dry season. After months without rain the Grumeti sometimes stops flowing and for many miles it may dry up completely, leaving only a sandy, tree-lined gully. When it rains in Africa, it rains really hard. As the wet season begins, thunderstorm follows thunderstorm, and flash floods sweep down the Grumeti. Only then, as it pours its muddy waters into Lake Victoria for the next few months, does it really deserve the name "river." It is like a thousand other little rivers on this great continent, and could easily be overlooked if it wasn't for something that makes the Grumeti very special—it is home to the largest crocodiles in Africa.

Grumeti crocodiles are Nile crocodiles, the largest kind in Africa. They can grow to over 20 feet (6 metres) long and weigh well over a ton. In the past, crocodiles were hunted for their skins, which were made into handbags and shoes. Since the largest were the easiest to find and were worth a lot more money, they were the first to be shot. Today, few are longer than 15 feet (about 4.5 metres). Although crocodiles are now protected by law, they grow very slowly, so it will be a long time before many grow to 20 feet (about 6 metres) again. The Grumeti crocodiles are especially safe because they live in the Serengeti National Park. On a 10-mile (16-kilometre) stretch of the river there are about a thousand crocodiles, from tiny babies to a giant old male who is almost 18 feet (5.5 metres) long. We have made our camp on this part of the river at a place called Kirawira. It takes its name from a poacher who swam across the river to escape the park rangers. He never reached the other side; and to this day the place where the largest crocodiles live is known as Kirawira.

Our story starts early one morning in May on the banks of the Grumeti. It is the end of the wet season and the river is swollen with muddy floodwater. The sandbanks are underwater, so the crocodiles have crowded together on a small island in the middle of the river to bask in the hot sun. Like all reptiles, crocodiles are said to be "cold-blooded," but this doesn't mean that a crocodile's blood is normally cold—it isn't. It's quite warm, like ours. This term just means that crocs can't generate their own body heat, so they need to lie in the sun to warm up. After a night in the river they are quite chilly, so as soon as the sun comes up, they haul themselves out and flop down for a few hours of sunbathing. If they stayed too long in the sun, they would overheat, so towards midday they either slip back into the water or crawl up into the shade. Most of their day is spent like this—either in and out of the water or in and out of the shade. It's a very relaxed lifestyle, and if you walk along the riverbank, it's tempting to think that all the crocodiles lying on the sandbanks are sleeping—but they aren't.

Like the Serengeti's lions, crocodiles are carnivores, which means they eat meat. Like lions, they too are hunters, but instead of chasing their prey, they ambush it. If an animal came down to drink, the apparently sleeping crocodile would slip quietly and slowly into the water and disappear. What happens next? Well, that comes later in the story.

Unlike humans, crocodiles cannot chew or break up food with their hands—so there is no point in a small crocodile trying to catch a large animal. It must catch what it can swallow whole. Baby crocodiles start off eating insects. In the heat of the day, if you are very quiet and still, you can see young crocs trying to sneak up on red dragonflies as they rest on reeds above the water. When the baby crocs grow a little bigger, they hunt freshwater crabs and frogs. After that it's fish, and only after they are full-grown adults will they be ready to eat the larger mammals.

It is later in the day now and most of the crocodiles that were sunbathing are warm enough to go fishing. At this time of year, fish are swimming upstream to spawn. The river is very muddy, so the crocs can't see the fish underwater—but they can feel them. They lie in the fast current with their jaws wide open, set like a trap. If a fish barely touches one of those teeth, the trap is sprung and the jaws crash together. It's a rather hit-or-miss style of hunting, but there's no chasing, and it doesn't require much energy—it's an ambush and that's what crocodiles do best. But what about the biggest crocs? They have been sitting on the riverbank all day. They don't seem interested in fishing, and no animals have come down to drink at the river. Well, we don't have to worry about them if they don't eat today, or this week, or even this month, because they are reptiles. Unlike people, large reptiles can live comfortably without feeding for several months after swallowing one big meal. Just imagine eating a large meal in December and then nothing else until April! How do the crocodiles do this? As we've seen, they conserve energy by resting most of the time, and the energy they need to keep warm comes from the sun instead of their food. This means that one large meal can keep a crocodile going for a long, long time.

The dry season begins in June, and now there is no more rain. Little by little the river starts to dry up. At first it's almost unnoticeable, but if you put a stick in the sand at water level at bedtime, in the morning you will see that the river has dropped almost an inch overnight.

As the plains alongside the river start to dry, the animals come to drink. But the big crocodiles still don't feed, because these animals have lived along-side the crocs all their lives and they are wary. They drink only where it is very shallow, so there is no chance of being ambushed.

One chilly morning something is different. We are used to the sounds and smells of the river—the raucous call of the fish-eagle or the bark of baboons if they are disturbed while picking tamarinds in the tree above our tent. This morning, though, it is still and strangely quiet.

The air is dusty and there is the faint smell of a farmyard. Then we hear a distant rumble. It sounds like a faraway jet or traffic on a busy road on the other side of a hill—but that's impossible in the Serengeti. It's the voices of a hundred thousand wildebeest.

Every year the great herds of wildebeest from the plains in the south of the Serengeti migrate northward in search of fresh grazing; and every year their journey brings them to the banks of the Grumeti River.

This is what the biggest crocs have been waiting for, and as the herds come to drink, the big crocs slip silently into the water and disappear. The wildebeest are hot and thirsty. There is no water left on the plains. Although they have been following the course of the river, before this point its banks have been lined with thick bush and thorn trees, so they have been unable to drink.

The calves are especially thirsty. They are tired from the long journey, and their mothers' milk is beginning to dry up. Even so, they do not rush down to the water, but stand beside their mothers at the top of the bank, bleating in anticipation.

With its head down to drink, legs splayed and feet firmly planted in the mud, a young wildebeest is easy game. A leopard or lion might be lurking in the bushes, so the wildebeest mill and jostle about nervously, each unwilling to be the first to go down to the water. Eventually an old bull, one-horned and limping, walks down to drink. Others follow, and soon the wildebeest line the bank shoulder to shoulder. The strangely shaped "logs" that come floating down with the current mean nothing to them. Even when those logs submerge, the wildebeest do not identify the threat.

Ever so slowly a pair of yellow eyes rises above the muddy water and then disappears. It happens so gradually that there is barely a ripple. The wildebeest notice nothing. Still the crocodiles do not attack. The water close to the bank is too shallow for a successful ambush.

The crocs have waited all year for this opportunity, so why attack too soon and risk frightening away the herd? So they wait...and wait. Then a wilde-beest steps farther out into the water. Maybe it was squashed between two others, or perhaps it did not like the muddy water closer to shore. Whatever the reason, that single step into deeper water is all the crocodile needs. He explodes from the water, his great jaws a blur as the wildebeest vanishes in the spray. It's all over in a matter of seconds.

A minute later the crocodile surfaces in midstream, the wildebeest already dead in its mouth. Other crocodiles have sensed the commotion and they hurry towards the disturbance. Ordinarily they would be too frightened to approach the large male that made the capture, but when there is food around, fear is forgotten. The large croc tolerates the others out of need, not generosity. Since crocodiles cannot chew, he cannot break up the body by himself. With lots of crocs hanging on, others can grab hold and then spin around and around to break pieces off.

Now and then a head emerges from the uproar. There is a toothy grin and a flash of white teeth as a chunk of meat is tossed back down the crocodile's throat.

Back on the bank the wildebeest have hardly noticed what has happened. They mill around but don't flee as they would from lions or hyenas. Those closest to the bank haven't even stopped drinking. Their confidence is contagious, and soon the herd is back drinking again.

For a week or so the crocodiles catch a wildebeest every day, and they grow fat and lazy. Very soon they don't even bother to hunt anymore, but lie in the sun sleeping off the huge meal. It's a real feast, but it's probably the only one the large crocodiles will have all year, because as suddenly as the wildebeest herd arrived, it disappears. They will have to make do with a few spiny catfish for twelve months, until the next dry season, when the wildebeest return.

At night now we lie awake and listen to the roars of the giant males as they challenge each other for ownership of the permanent pools. One night there is a terrible fight as two males chase each other along the riverbed beside our camp. In the moonlight we see them wrestle and bite each other in the struggle for dominance. Towards morning the newcomer is driven from the pool and the victorious old male slaps his great jaws together in a prehistoric sound that echoes along the river. This fight was unusual, for normally such contests are settled long before they erupt into violence. As long as the others acknowledge the supremacy of the old male, he will not attack, and the crocodile pool is a surprisingly peaceful and sociable place.

The prospect of a permanent pool with its resident female crocodiles means that the younger male will be back, though perhaps not this year. The old male in the pool near our camp is almost 100 years old and has been king of this stretch of river for perhaps 20 years.

He is almost 18 feet (5.5 metres) long and his massive head is heavily ridged and knobbed. When he hauls himself out of the water and lumbers out onto the sandbank, he stands nearly 3 feet (about 1 metre) high. He has fought off many challengers over the years, and while he shows no scars of combat, others are less lucky. The crocodile in the next pool downstream has lost the end of his top jaw—most likely from a battle with another crocodile.

When we walk down to the pool from our camp, the old male is always the first crocodile we see as he basks or patrols his pool. The females are harder to see, for at this time of year they lie hidden, up in the bushes guarding their nests. Almost 3 months ago the females laid their eggs. Each dug a hole a couple of feet deep and then laid anywhere from 30 to 90 eggs roughly the size of goose eggs, with hard white shells. Once the sand had been replaced, there was nothing to show where the eggs were.

For the next three months the females stay close by, to guard their eggs against hyenas, baboons, and monitor lizards. The monitor lizards are the biggest threat, for they constantly dig test holes up and down the beach, prospecting for eggs.

If a female leaves for even a few minutes, the 3-foot (1 metre) lizards will scuttle in and start digging. Occasionally one is lucky and emerges with an egg in its mouth. Usually, once the nest has been opened it is doomed, because mongooses and baboons will not be far behind.

We have to be careful not to disturb the nesting females, so we stay hidden from view inside a canvas hide, waiting for the eggs to hatch.

At dawn one morning, as we are getting into the hide for the day, we hear a strange noise. It is a muted squeaking, which we hear only when we move. It's very strange—if we stop, it stops. Walking gently over to the nest, we press our ears to the ground and tap the sand. Immediately we are answered by a chorus of tiny squeaks. It's the baby crocodiles calling to their mother! After 3 months in the hot sun, the sand above the nest has baked hard. It's too hard for the baby crocodiles to wriggle through on their own, so now that they are ready to hatch, they are calling their mother to come and release them.

As soon as we are settled in the hide, the mother crocodile emerges from the water. Lying on top of the nest, she starts to dig down with her front feet. It's tiring work and she rests often. With every clawful of sand she clears, the squeaking gets louder. At last, driven on by the cries of her babies, she uncovers the first egg. It hatches instantly, and a perfect miniature crocodile crawls out. It's about 10 inches (25 centimetres) long, and it calls, "Eeoww. Eeoww, eeoww." Try it—it's a short, high-pitched sound. Run the "ee" and the "oww" together, and as you do it, wrinkle up your nose and draw your top lip back—that's the sound that the baby crocodiles make.

As other eggs are uncovered, they also hatch, and soon a small group of babies has collected around the female. Then something extraordinary happens. She looks down and starts to take them into her mouth. At first it appears she is going to eat them, but she doesn't. Very carefully she puts the babies in her mouth. She throws some of them into the air and catches them with the same movement used to eat pieces of meat. (Look carefully at the photo on the opposite page—just in front of the lower jaw of the mother with her mouth open, one of her babies is in midair.) She doesn't swallow them, but the floor of her mouth drops to form a pouch. Before long there are a dozen tiny crocodiles peering out from behind those enormous teeth. They look like prisoners behind bars, but they are inside for their own protection. Once their mother has a mouthful, she carries them down over the beach to the safety of the water. There she releases them close to the reeds.

Back at the nest the predators have homed in, and many of the babies are taken by monitors, eagles, and mongooses before the mother returns. Of the 30 eggs she laid, only 20 tiny crocodiles make it as far as the river. Even there they are not completely safe.

If they stray into deep water, they are in danger of being eaten by large fish such as catfish or the giant Nile perch shown here. They hide in the reeds, but even so there is constant danger from hungry storks, eagles, and snakes.

For the next few weeks the mother will stay close to her babies to guard them. She is a very caring parent, and when she lifts her head above the water, all the babies scramble to get on top, because it's the safest place in the river.

Even when one steps on her eye as it climbs up, she only blinks in a good-natured way. She is very tolerant of this pile of wriggling babies, but eventually even the patience of a crocodile is strained, and she slips below the surface to gain a moment's peace. This upsets her babies, who aren't so used to the water. They are left splashing and rolling around in confusion. As soon as she appears, though, it all starts again, and for the next few weeks she won't get any peace.

But no matter how watchful their mother is, she can't guard all her babies all the time. Some get lost or eaten, others are washed away by the river, and a few weeks after her babies have hatched, only 5 or 6 remain.

It's time for them to set off on their own now, to hunt for themselves and slowly learn the skills they will need if they are going to survive to become adults.

The little ones need to discover what they might eat—and what might eat them—and learn that hippos and even big crocodiles are no friends of small crocodiles. They must find out where to go if the river dries up. Already they have made a good start.

As we watch them jumping up at the red dragonflies that rest on the reeds, we can see them already developing the skills they will need for the rest of their lives. And although they don't know it, the way they are learning to catch dragonflies today—the slow stalk and sudden strike—is the same ambush they will use in 30 years' time, when they are big enough to catch wildebeest.

As dusk falls and we prepare to go back to our camp, we take one last look around, using flashlights. If we hold our lights alongside our heads, we can see the reflections of the eyes of the baby crocodiles, like so many glowing coals, from their hiding places close to the bank.

They have a long way to go, but perhaps one will make it. Perhaps if your grandchildren come to these pools on the Grumeti in 80 years' time and see a giant male crocodile who rules the river—who knows? He might be one of those tiny babies we saw carried down to the water, so gently, all those years ago.

The Animal Family Series

The Animal Family books are not just written by their authors. They are studied and researched and lived into existence. When the authors travel around the world to study, children go right along with them, profiting from the naturalists' firsthand knowledge and experiences in the field. Each book in the Animal Family series helps to make the world of nature that much more real, more understandable, and more valuable to children everywhere.

Ask your bookseller for these other Animal Family books:

THE BEAVER FAMILY BOOK
THE CHIMPANZEE FAMILY BOOK
THE DESERT FOX FAMILY BOOK
THE ELEPHANT FAMILY BOOK
THE GOOSE FAMILY BOOK
THE GRIZZLY BEAR FAMILY BOOK
THE LEOPARD FAMILY BOOK
THE LION FAMILY BOOK
THE PENGUIN FAMILY BOOK
THE POLAR BEAR FAMILY BOOK
THE WHALE FAMILY BOOK
THE WILD HORSE FAMILY BOOK